A Scottish YEAR

FOR NARELLE. MÓRAN TAING. –TS
FOR WILLIAM. FROM SCOTLAND TO TASMANIA, MANY YEARS AGO. –TM

A Scottish YEAR

TWELVE MONTHS IN THE LIFE OF SCOTLAND'S KIDS

TANIA McCARTNEY + TINA SNERLING

EK

Welcome to Scotland

SAY CHEESE!

Hello, I'm RASHIDA and I arrived from Pakistan when I was just three. I'm now ten. I love my iPad, animals, and playing my violin. When I grow up, I want to be a zoologist.

Hiya, I'm SOPHIE and I'm seven. I like sewing clothes for my dolls, playing tennis and seeing wildflowers in the Highlands. When I'm older, I hope to become a fashion designer.

Witam! I'm DOMINIK and I'm eight years old. My parents were born in Poland. I think science is really cool and I love the planets and stars. I'd like to be an astronaut.

Hi, I'm ISLA and I come from a very old Scottish family. I'm six years old and I love dancing, drawing and baking with Mum. When I grow up, I want to be a famous artist.

Awrite! I'm JAMES. I'm nine and I'm a football fanatic! I love playing on the computer and going camping and hiking. I like being out in nature and I want to be a fireman one day.

January

January is cold and WET and snowy. It's Baltic!

It's NEW YEAR'S DAY! It used to be called Ne'er Day.

We have another PUBLIC holiday.

WHISKY

BLACK BUN

COAL

SHORTBREAD

Our neighbour arrives to FIRST FOOT us. He carries presents to bring good luck.

It's TWELFTH NIGHT. We take down our Christmas tree to avoid bad luck.

We go ice skating and sledging, and have SNOWBALL fights, too.

xmas decorations

We have TEA around the family table.

BEEF KARAHI

BEANS AND CHIPS

MINCE AND TATTIES

STOVIES

CHICKEN NUGGETS

MACARONI CHEESE

Celtic Connections in Glasgow ROCKS!

It's back to SCHOOL. We're half way through the school year.

THIS WAY TO SCHOOL

We walk, RIDE our bikes or get a lift to school.

We write poems in SCOTS at school.

Poems in Scots by James

ALSO CALLED BURNS' NICHT

We celebrate BURNS' NIGHT with haggis, neeps and tatties.

MADE IN HAGGIS SCOTLAND

February

Six Nations RUGBY begins.

On cold days, we love eating SCONES, hot from the oven.

Dad makes square SAUSAGE butties.

At the weekend, some of us go SKIING.

GOOD THOUGHTS

22

It's PANCAKE Day. We flip pancakes high in the air.

It's WORLD THINKING DAY for Girl Guides and Girl Scouts.

Up Helly Aa is ABLAZE with fire!

At PLAYTIME we have lots of fun!

HOPSCOTCH

MANHUNT

SHARK ATTACK

FOOTBALL

We have loads to keep us busy after SCHOOL.

LEGO

HOMEWORK

WALK THE DOG

GYMNASTICS

On VALENTINE'S DAY, we get cards from a secret admirer.

CLANG!

POP!

CHINESE NEW YEAR is very noisy!
Sometimes it falls in January.

March

We go FISHING in the burn with Grandpa.

INVERNESS Music Festival.

On the weekends, we RIDE HORSES, play football with Dad or go for the messages with Mum.

The bulbs in our garden are starting to SPROUT.

It's COMMONWEALTH Day.

BREAKFAST

GIFTS

CARDS

On MOTHER'S DAY, we spoil Mum with breakfast in bed, gifts and cards.

At school, we raise funds for RED NOSE DAY.

British SUMMER Time begins.

CLOCKS GO FORWARD

Our SCOTTISH TERRIERS love to run in the woods.

SNOWDROPS and baby lambs are everywhere!

It's EARTH HOUR. We turn off the lights because we care for our planet.

EARTH HOUR

April

It's APRIL FOOLS' DAY. We have until midday to play tricks on each other!

IT USED TO BE CALLED HUNTIGOWK DAY.

At Easter time, we love HOT CROSS BUNS with butter.

It's CLEAN UP Scotland's Spring Clean.

We have SPRING holidays for Easter.

EGG HUNT

We bairns love to paint EGGS. We roll them down the nearest hill.

On EASTER SUNDAY, we hunt for chocolate eggs then eat roast lamb for dinner.

HERBS grow on the kitchen window sill.

parsley   basil   rosemary

TARTAN DAY celebrates everything good about Scotland!

6

We love to play GAMES on the telly, and on iPads and computers.

We go to the seaside and stay in a CARAVAN.

DRUMS

MUSIC

FIRE

Crocuses, DAFFODILS and bluebells abound.

The Beltane FIRE Festival celebrates the arrival of summer.

May

1

On MAY DAY, we have a day off school.

We ride the JACOBITE steam train to Mallaig.

YOGHURT

PIECES

CURRY

CRISPS

WRAP

We take our lunch to school or eat in the DINNER HALL.

The IMAGINATE Festival is brilliant fun for kids!

We slurp milkshakes and drink ginger, like IRN-BRU.

We spot dolphins and SEALS on the Moray Firth.

It's WARMING up. We play golf or go to an indoor pool.

THISTLES start blooming on the hills near our house.

We just love our SWEETIES!

TABLET

GUMMY BEARS

HUMBUGS

PAN DROPS

EDINBURGH ROCK

MIX-UP

BUTTERSCOTCH

QUEEN

Queen Victoria's birthday is remembered on VICTORIA DAY.

PUFFINS and gannets can be seen on Bass Rock.

June

Time to head outdoors for a PICNIC.

It's SUMMER. The midges arrive!

We go CAMPING in the Highlands.

We celebrate the Queen's BIRTHDAY.

It's the Royal HIGHLAND SHOW.

LUPINS

MARIGOLDS

ROSEBAY WILLOWHERB

COWSLIP

BINDWEED

We love the Glasgow SCIENCE Festival.

WILDFLOWERS coat the hillsides.

As the weather HEATS UP,
we get out the paddling pool.

Scotland has some of the most beautiful CASTLES in the world.

Granny makes us DUNDEE Cake.

We play ROUNDERS in the summer sun.

The summer HOLIDAYS begin!

It's FATHER'S DAY and we love to spoil our dad.

July

We go hillwalking and MOO at the Highland cows.

We take over the kitchen and bake up some TREATS.

FAIRY CAKES CARROT CAKE COOKIES

FLOUR

We pick blaeberries and MUNCH them before tea.

FOUR!

Mum GROWS potatoes, leeks and carrots in our vegetable garden.

Dad takes us GOLFING.

August

The school year **BEGINS**.

SHIRT

TIE

BLAZER

POLO SHIRT

SWEATSHIRT

TROUSERS

LAMMAS celebrates the first harvest of the year.

It's International **YOUTH** Day.

12

The **FOOTBALL** season begins!

We watch the Royal Edinburgh **MILITARY TATTOO** on the telly.

At bedtime, it's still **LIGHT** outside!

I HOPE THEY CAN'T SEE US!

It's the **GLORIOUS** Twelfth.

Heather on the hills is in full BLOOM.

People toss cabers and throw hammers at the Cowal HIGHLAND GATHERING.

The UNICORN is the official animal of Scotland.

It's SHINTY season.

During the holidays, we go PONY trekking on the Isle of Skye.

The Edinburgh Festival is awesome. We dive into stories at the BOOK FESTIVAL.

September

AUTUMN is here.

CRUMPETS WITH JAM

PARATHA FRIED BREAD AND YOGHURT

SAUSAGES, EGGS AND BAKED BEANS

TATTIE SCONES

PORRIDGE

We slip on our WELLIES and jump in puddles.

For BREAKFAST, we eat many different things. At the weekend, Dad likes a fry-up.

It's the BRAEMAR Gathering.

CYCLING is one of our favourite things to do. We ride along the Forth and Clyde Canal.

We pick raspberres and brambles. Mum makes a PIE.

We love a POKE of chips.

The street is a GREAT place to kick a ball.

Deer, foxes and wildcats run FREE on the hills.

TARTAN is worn to celebrate our clan.

We search for NESSIE at Loch Ness.

 **OCtOBeR**

It's wet and windy and really **DREICH.**

British Summer **TIME** ends.

CLOCKS GO BACK

It's **WORLD TEACHERS' DAY.**

We spot GOLDEN EAGLES circling high in the sky.

We kick up **LEAVES** and pick chestnuts.

As the weather cools down,
Grandpa likes a **HOT TODDY** at bedtime.

The An Fhèis Mhòr festival of PADDLESPORT is a lot of watery fun.

It's October mid-term break. We call it TATTIE WEEK.

COLD ENOUGH FOR YOU?

Geese and swans ARRIVE for the winter.

We celebrate GAELIC music, arts and culture at the Mòd festival.

At HALLOWE'EN, we dress up and go guising. We sing, tell jokes or recite poems for sweeties and fruit.

We put on our coats and play CONKERS outdoors.

NOVEMBER

5

On GUY FAWKES NIGHT, we watch fireworks and wave sparklers in the night sky.

We write our Christmas list and throw it up the CHIMNEY.

It's almost TOO COLD to go on the trampoline!

EAR MUFFS

COAT

MITTENS

SKATES

We go CURLING at the ice rink.

We love warm PORRIDGE on cold mornings.

BROWN SUGAR

STIR CLOCKWISE

CREAM

SPURTLE

People ICE SKATE at the Oban Winter Festival.

We skim pebbles on the LOCH before it freezes over for winter.

It's REMEMBRANCE DAY. We remember our soldiers by wearing red poppies.

11

Lest We Forget

We PRACTISE football, hockey and rugby after school.

It's UNIVERSAL CHILDREN'S DAY.

20

We celebrate ST ANDREW'S DAY with singing and dancing. Saltires fly at ceilidhs all over the country.

30

We're on the lookout for red SQUIRRELS!

December

WINTER creeps in.

We start opening the little doors and windows on our ADVENT calendars.

Towns everywhere switch on their CHRISTMAS LIGHTS.

VERY IMPORTANT DAY
10
It's HUMAN RIGHTS DAY.

STAR

TARTAN RIBBON

TINSEL

PAPER CHAINS

WREATH MADE OF HOLLY

It's Christmas holidays. We visit the local Christmas market and see SANTA in his grotto.

Our Christmas TREE is native Scots pine.

On Christmas Eve, we hang STOCKINGS on the end of our beds.

CHRISTMAS EVE USED TO BE CALLED SOWANS NICHT.

CHRISTMAS DINNER is delicious!

We giggle our heads off at the local PANTOMIME.

On BOXING DAY, we eat all the leftovers!

22

It's the SHORTEST DAY of the year!

PIGS IN BLANKETS

CLOOTIE DUMPLING

TURKEY

ROAST POTATOES

MASHED NEEPS AND TATTIES

CRANACHAN

CHRISTMAS PUDDING

Everyone helps with REDDING the house, to bring in a fresh new year.

It's HOGMANAY! We nibble shortbread and toast the bells with lemonade. Everyone sings Auld Lang Syne to farewell another grand year.

Our Country

THE REGIONS OF SCOTLAND

Aberdeen City and Shire
Argyll and The Isles
Ayrshire and Arran
Dumfries and Galloway
Dundee and Angus
Edinburgh and the The Lothians
Greater Glasgow and The Clyde Valley
The Highlands
The Kingdom of Fife
Loch Lomond, The Trossachs, Stirling and Forth Valley
Orkney
Outer Hebrides
Perthshire
The Scottish Borders
Shetland

SCOTLAND HAS OVER 790 ISLANDS

We have around 2000 CASTLES! That's a lot!

Scotland abounds in natural beauty.

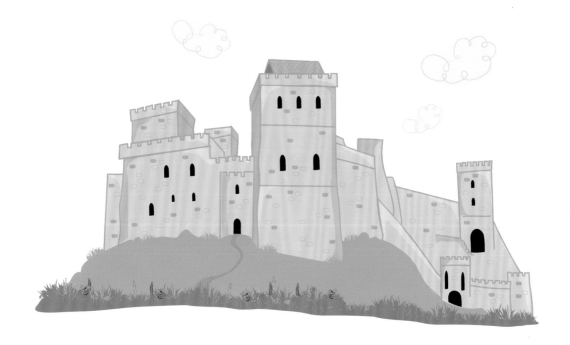

A huge thank you to Scottish advisors Pam Gregory and Maureen Johnson, and to the kids of Cambusbarron Primary School. Also to the team at Exisle and our publisher Anouska Jones for her insight and eagle editing eye. — TM + TS

First published 2015

EK Books
an imprint of Exisle Publishing Pty Ltd
Inverwick House, Albert Street, Nairn,
IV12 4HE, Scotland, UK
'Moonrising', Narone Creek Road,
Wollombi, NSW 2325, Australia
P.O. Box 60-490, Titirangi
Auckland 0642, New Zealand
www.ekbooks.com.au

A CiP record for this book is available from the National Library of Australia

ISBN 978 1 921966 87 3

Designed and typeset by Tina Snerling
Typeset in Century Gothic, Street Cred and custom fonts
Printed in China
This book uses paper sourced under ISO 1 4001 guidelines from well-managed forests and other controlled sources.

10 9 8 7 6 5 4 3 2 1

Author Note

This is by no means a comprehensive listing of the events and traditions celebrated by Scotland's multitude of ethnic people. The entries in this book have been chosen to reflect a range of modern lifestyles for the majority of Scottish children, with a focus on traditional 'Scottish' elements and themes, which are in themselves a glorious mishmash of present, past, introduced and endemic culture. Content in this book has been produced in consultation with native Scottish advisors, school teachers, and school children, with every intention of respecting the cultural and idiosyncratic elements of Scotland and its people.